# Lola
## the Fashion Show
## Fairy

by Daisy Meadows

ORCHARD

**www.rainbowmagic.co.uk**

The Fairyland Palace

Tippington Fountains SHOPPING CENTRE

Fashion Show

Top heels & tiaras

HARTLEYS

"Ice Blue" Hair Salon

TIPPINGTON TOYS

"Ice Blue" stall

Jack Frost's
Ice Castle

Up to the
Roof Garden
Cafe

LIFT

ant.

Wishing
Town

COMFY FEET

Ice cream
parlour

WINTER WOOLIES

Beautiful YOU!

SNIP & CUP

Central
fountain

Press
booth

Bath Bliss

Jack Frost's Spell

I'm the king of designer fashion,
Looking stylish is my passion.
Ice Blue's the name of my fashion range,
Some people think my clothes are strange.

Do I care, though? Not a bit!
My designer label will be a hit.
The Fashion Fairies' magic will make that come true:
Soon everyone will wear Ice Blue!

# Contents

## Off to
## the Show

Kirsty Tate was *very* excited. Today, she and her best friend Rachel Walker were taking part in a fashion show! Not only that, they would be wearing outfits they had designed and made themselves, after entering a special competition held at *Tippington Fountains Shopping Centre* earlier that week.

"I hope I don't trip over on the catwalk," Rachel giggled as she, Kirsty and her parents walked to their meeting point in the shopping centre. "Knowing me, I'll fall flat on my face and totally embarrass myself."

"No, you won't," Kirsty reassured her, squeezing her hand. "You'll be brilliant. And everyone will love your rainbow jeans, I just know it."

Rachel smiled at her. "I'm so glad we're doing this together," she said.

"Me too." Kirsty grinned. "All of our best adventures happen when we're together, don't they?"

The two girls exchanged a look, their eyes sparkling. Unknown to anyone else, they shared an amazing secret. They were friends with the fairies, and had enjoyed lots of wonderful, magical fairy adventures with them. Sometimes, the girls had even been turned into fairies themselves, and been able to fly!

This week, Kirsty was staying with Rachel's family for half-term and once again, the two friends had found themselves magically whisked away to Fairyland when a brand-new fairy adventure began. They'd been invited to see a fairy fashion show but unfortunately it had been hijacked by naughty Jack Frost and his goblin servants, who barged in, all wearing outfits from Jack Frost's new designer label, Ice Blue. Jack Frost had declared that everyone should wear his range of clothes, so they'd all look like him! Then, with a crackling bolt of icy magic, he had stolen the Fashion Fairies' seven magical objects and vanished into the human world.

The Fashion Fairies were horrified. They needed their special magical objects to make sure that everyone's clothes and accessories fitted perfectly and that fashion shows everywhere were successful. Now that Jack Frost had taken these objects, all sorts of things could go wrong!

Kirsty and Rachel had been busily tracking down and returning the fairies' stolen objects, and so far they had found six of them. There was still one missing, though, and it belonged to Lola the Fashion Show Fairy.

"Here we are," said Rachel's mum.

"Goodness, look at that catwalk! I can't believe you two will be walking along there later on."

Rachel and Kirsty fell silent as they gazed at the scene before them. *Tippington Fountains Shopping Centre* had only opened this week and everything still sparkled with newness: the glass shop fronts, the chrome fittings and the magnificent central fountain display. In front of the fountain was a long catwalk with rows of seats on either side.

Kirsty swallowed, feeling nervous for the first time that day.

"I really hope we can help Lola find her magic object before the show starts," she whispered to Rachel.

"Me too," Rachel replied, crossing her fingers. Her heart quickened as she imagined all the seats filled with people watching the show. If she and Kirsty couldn't find Lola's magic object in time, it could turn out to be the worst fashion show ever!

# Fairy Lights

"Hello there, girls!"

Kirsty and Rachel turned to see Jessica Jarvis standing behind them. Jessica was the supermodel who had taken part in the shopping centre's fun events that week.

"I'm glad to see some more guest models have arrived," said Jessica, smiling.

Kirsty frowned and gazed around, wondering where the guest models were – until Rachel nudged her. "*We're* the guest models," she giggled. "Jessica is talking about us!"

"Oh! Hi, Jessica!" Kirsty said, blushing.

Jessica introduced herself to Rachel's parents and promised she'd keep an eye on the girls. "I'll make sure there are some seats reserved in the front row for you," she added.

"Thank you," Mrs Walker said, hugging Rachel, then Kirsty. "I can't wait to see you in action. Enjoy yourselves!"

"See you later, girls," Mr Walker said. "Good luck!"

Once Mr and Mrs Walker had left, Jessica sorted out special backstage passes for the girls. The passes were in plastic sleeves on long loops of ribbon, which the girls pulled over their heads.

Then Jessica took them backstage and into the dressing area. This was a large room with dressing tables, rails of outfits, and swivel chairs in front of brightly lit mirrors. Dean and Layla, the other two winners of the Design-and-Make Competition, were having their hair styled, and other models were having make-up applied.

"Wow," Rachel breathed, gazing
around. The fashion show suddenly felt
much more real now that they could see
everyone getting ready.

"I've got tingles,"
Kirsty said, with a
rush of excitement
as she spotted
the floaty dress
she'd made
hanging up
with the other
outfits. She'd
carefully stitched
together lots of
brightly coloured scarves
in order to make the dress, while Rachel
had decorated her jeans with a rainbow
pattern using glittery paint. Layla was

already wearing the stylish football kit she had designed, and Dean had on his space-themed T-shirt and a pair of smart jeans. The hairdresser was putting sticky-looking gel into Dean's hair and teasing it forward into a space-age quiff.

"Fabulous," Jessica said admiringly, then turned to Kirsty and Rachel. "Girls, why don't you change into your outfits? Then we can talk about catwalk order. I was wondering, as you two are friends, if you'd like to walk down the catwalk together?"

"Yes, please," Rachel said at once. She knew she'd feel much more confident with Kirsty next to her.

"That would be brilliant," Kirsty agreed. "Come on, Rachel, let's get changed."

Jessica went to speak to Dean and

Layla while the girls took their outfits
and went to a quiet corner to put them
on. There was a mirror nearby with
spotlights shining all around it and, as
Rachel glanced at it to check that her
rainbow jeans looked OK, she noticed
that one of the lights seemed to gleam
brighter than all the others. How strange!

She leaned closer to investigate…then
gasped as a tiny fairy fluttered down
from where she'd been hiding beside
the light. *That* was why it had shone so
brightly!

"Kirsty!"
Rachel hissed,
her skin
prickling with
excitement.
"Come and see!"

Kirsty finished pulling on her scarf-dress and hurried over, beaming as she too saw the little fairy.

"Hello," said the fairy, landing lightly on Rachel's hand. "I'm Lola the Fashion Show Fairy. It's nice to see you two again!"

"Hello, Lola," Rachel replied, twisting her body slightly so that the fairy was shielded from view. "Have you seen your magical object anywhere?"

Lola shook her head. She had long red wavy hair that fell around her face, and wore a silvery mini-dress and long

silver boots. She pointed to the pass she
wore around her neck, just like the girls'
backstage passes. The only difference was,
her plastic sleeve was empty.

"I really need to find my magical pass
before the show begins," she said, biting
her lip. "Otherwise this show – and others
like it everywhere – will be ruined!"

Just then, Jessica called the girls over. "Right, I'm going to take Dean, Layla and the other models through to the rehearsal area," she said. "I'll send someone to do your hair and make-up in a few minutes."

"Thanks," Kirsty replied politely. The other models followed Jessica, leaving the room empty except for the two friends and Lola.

Moments later, the door crashed open.
Startled, Lola hid in a fold of Kirsty's
dress as three boys burst in with armfuls
of blue clothes, a make-up kit and an
enormous basket of accessories. The boys
were all dressed alike in crazy bright-
blue outfits and large blue hats with wide
brims covering their faces.

"Move out of my way! I said, MOVE!"
boomed a bossy voice, and in strode a
taller figure with a bright-blue furry coat

and large blue sunglasses. "The star has arrived!" he announced with a smirk.

The air seemed to turn cold with the new arrivals and Kirsty felt a shiver run through her as she realised who they were: Jack Frost and his goblins!

# A Frosty Encounter

Rachel clutched Kirsty's arm as she too recognised Jack Frost and his gang. What are *they* doing here, she thought in alarm, as one of the goblins locked the door behind them.

"We'll get rid of these awful clothes for a start," Jack Frost declared, busily dumping the remaining outfits on the rail onto the floor. Then he carefully arranged his own Ice Blue garments in their place. "That's better."

The goblins, meanwhile, were sweeping all the make-up and accessories off the dressing tables. Powder spilled on the jewellery, lipsticks smeared the pale carpet, and perfume bottles smashed, releasing a mix of clashing scents into the air.

"We won't need those any more," said the goblins. They smirked as they unpacked the basket of make-up and accessories they'd brought – all bright blue, of course.

Lola gasped in surprise as she spotted something. "Look! My pass!" she whispered. "Jack Frost is wearing it around his neck!"

Thinking quickly, Rachel pulled Kirsty behind the rail of Ice Blue clothes before Jack Frost noticed them. They peeped out to see him settling himself into a chair in front of the biggest mirror and shouting orders to his goblins as to how to style his hair.

"Lola, please could you turn me and Kirsty into fairies?" Rachel whispered. "We can try to fly over and grab your pass while Jack Frost's distracted."

"Good idea," Lola replied, raising her wand. She pointed it at the girls then waved it in an elaborate pattern, murmuring some magic words under her breath. There was a bright flash of silver light and then a flurry of twinkling sparkles glittered all around the girls.

Seconds later, they felt themselves shrinking smaller and smaller until they were the same size as Lola. Kirsty beamed as she saw that she and Rachel now had their own shimmering fairy wings. How she loved being a fairy!

The three friends flew carefully around the end of the clothing rail and watched. The goblins were busily powdering Jack Frost's face and using hair gel to make his long beard even spikier than ever.

"Get a move on," he snapped at them crossly. "We haven't got all day!"

Just then, somebody tried to come into the room. "How strange. It's locked!" the girls heard from outside as the handle was turned and twisted. Then came a knocking at the door. "Hello? Is anyone there? We've come to do hair and make-up for our last two models!"

Jack Frost's top lip curled. "You're not needed any more," he shouted in reply. "The other models have changed their minds about appearing in my show." He cackled. "There'll only be one model today," he said in a lower voice to his reflection. "The most handsome one in the world...

wearing the very best clothes. Soon
everyone will know *my* name!"

Kirsty and Rachel exchanged a
worried glance as the hair and make-up
people went away. Oh no, this was all
going badly wrong! And yet there was
the magic pass gleaming and glimmering
as it hung on Jack Frost's chest. If only
they could get hold of it!

"Let's make a grab for my pass," said
Lola, and she shot out from their hiding
place at top speed. She dived
towards her magic pass,
hand outstretched,
but at the last
moment Jack
Frost caught
sight of her in
the mirror.

"Oh no you don't!" he cried, twisting quickly so that the swivel chair spun him and the pass out of Lola's reach.

Kirsty and Rachel tried a different approach, swooping around the back of the chair in their attempts to get the pass. But again, Jack Frost swung the chair so that it whizzed away before they could reach.

"Wretched fairies!" he grumbled, batting at the air with his hands. "Don't you know I've a fashion show to star in?"

Lola gritted her teeth. "It would be an even better show if you gave me back my pass," she pointed out.

"Not a chance!" retorted Jack Frost, spinning the chair round so fast that the goblins had to chase after him with the hair gel and face powder.

The fairies flew after him too, swooping in circles as he spun the chair. He was

starting to look dizzy, Kirsty noticed. If he became much dizzier, he might not notice her grab the magic pass!

She whispered her idea to the other two and they agreed that they'd try to make Jack Frost as dizzy as possible. Round and round they all flew, occasionally

darting in to make a grab at Lola's pass, which caused him to spin the chair even faster. He sagged in the chair, his face becoming as green as a goblin's, and Kirsty decided that this was her best chance. She took a deep breath. It was now or never. She had to snatch the magic pass!

# Mirror, Mirror

Down flew Kirsty, her eyes on Lola's magic pass...but just before she could reach it, Jack Frost suddenly staggered out of the chair and lurched across the floor. He was so dizzy that he fell into the clothes rails, sending them toppling over with a crash.

Rachel winced at the noise. Surely any minute now someone would come and want to know what was going on in the dressing area! And how much time did they have before the fashion show was due to start, anyway? Soon the audience would be taking their seats, anticipating a wonderful event...only for Jack Frost to wreck the whole thing. They had to stop him!

She, Kirsty and Lola fluttered high in the air as Jack Frost lunged for the dressing area door, unlocked it and staggered out. They

followed him down the corridor to the curtained entrance of the catwalk.

"Excuse me, sir, you're not meant to—" a steward said in surprise, but it was too late to stop Jack Frost. He blundered dizzily through the curtains, grabbing hold of them for support. Then he lunged onto the catwalk, pulling the curtains down with him!

The curtain rail crashed onto the podium and the catwalk, and the lighting stands immediately tipped over. Jack Frost let out a shout of rage as he wrenched the curtain off himself and emerged, rubbing his head. He scowled at the goblins. "Sort this mess out at once!" he snapped.

The three fairy friends could only stare open-mouthed at the chaos Jack Frost was causing.

"If I had my magic pass, I could make all of this look like new in an instant," groaned Lola as the crew began trying to repair the catwalk, helped by the goblins. "We simply must get it back before the fashion show starts. What can we do?"

Thinking hard, the fairies followed Jack Frost, who'd stalked away. His pass swung to and fro as he walked and Rachel noticed that as he turned a corner, the pass swung out to the side. Then, seeing a deserted corridor, she had an idea.

"Lola, would you be able to use your magic to conjure up mirrors down the sides of this corridor, and one at the end?" she asked.

Lola nodded. "Of course," she said. "Why?"

Rachel smiled. "I've got an idea," she said, and whispered it to them.

"That might just work," Kirsty said. "And there's no time to lose. Come on, let's try it!"

Lola waved her wand and turned Rachel and Kirsty back into girls.

Then she waved her
wand a second
time, and a whole
row of mirrors
appeared along
the corridor,
with an extra-
large one at the
end. Now to set
the plan in action!

"I heard that
someone from the
Gorgeous Model Agency is going to be
here today," Rachel said in a very loud
voice. "Apparently they're hunting for a
new supermodel."

"We should definitely practise for the
catwalk," Kirsty replied, just as loudly.
"This is the perfect spot."

The two girls began walking the length of the corridor, pretending it was a catwalk. When they reached the enormous mirror at the end, they twirled around, causing their backstage passes to swing to the side. All the while, they talked in loud voices about how much they hoped they'd be picked as the next supermodel. Really, of course, they were just hoping Jack Frost would overhear them and come to find out more.

Sure enough, within a few moments Jack Frost appeared with his goblins. Lola, who was perched up high on a chandelier overlooking the corridor, peered down with excitement.

"If anyone's going to be picked as the next supermodel, it's *me*," Jack Frost said grandly. "Move aside, girls. Even a star like me needs to practise sometimes, and this looks the perfect place to do it."

Jack Frost began to strut down the corridor, admiring himself in the mirrors.

Then, when he reached the big mirror at the end of the corridor, the girls and Lola held their breath. If all went to plan, he would twirl around, his pass would swing out and Lola would be able to grab it.

He began to turn, and Lola swooped
down from the chandelier, her eyes fixed
on the pass. This time their plan *had* to
work!

# Twirl, and Twirl Again

Unfortunately, Jack Frost stopped, mid-twirl, to gaze lovingly at himself in the mirror. This meant that his pass didn't swing out very far at all…and Lola had to quickly loop-the-loop and soar back to her hiding place in dismay. Oh no. Foiled again!

"Perfect," Jack Frost declared with a smirk, as he finished his turn and set off back down the corridor. The goblins watched admiringly. One even clapped.

Kirsty thought quickly. "You know, I've heard that you should do a really big, dramatic twirl at the end of the catwalk, if you want the agency to notice you," she said to Rachel. "I'm going to practise that now, I think."

"No, you're not," Jack Frost told her. "Get off my catwalk, you silly girl. This is my practice time now, and *I'm* going to do the biggest and most dramatic twirl anyone has ever seen!"

Rachel winked at Kirsty. "Hmmm, I'm not sure he'll be able to do a *really* big twirl," she said dismissively.

Jack Frost bristled in annoyance. "Well, watch this," he snapped. "Prepare to be *dazzled* by my twirl!"

Once again, Kirsty, Rachel and Lola all held their breath as Jack Frost neared the end of the corridor. Approaching the big mirror, he whipped around in the most exaggerated twirl ever, sending his pass flying out horizontally from his body. In the blink of an eye, Lola whizzed down at lightning speed, and plucked her pass straight from the plastic sleeve. It shrank down to fairy size and she flew away with it, laughing in delight.

Jack Frost looked so furious, Rachel
and Kirsty thought he might explode.
"That's mine!" he yelled.
"Give that back!"

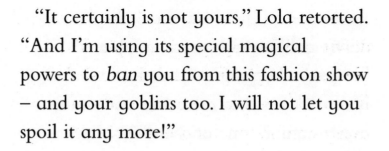

"It certainly is not yours," Lola retorted.
"And I'm using its special magical
powers to *ban* you from this fashion show
– and your goblins too. I will not let you
spoil it any more!"

Jack Frost stamped his foot but he knew he was powerless against the magic of Lola's pass. Now that she had it back, she could use it to make all fashion shows run perfectly – which meant he was unable to stay. "Well, it's your loss," he sulked. "I'll go back to my Ice Castle and keep my Ice Blue designs all to myself from now on. And then you'll be sorry!"

The goblins looked rather pleased. "If you're keeping your designs to yourself does that mean we can wear green again?" one of them asked.

He lifted his blue top to reveal a green
T-shirt underneath, with GOBLINS
ROCK! embroidered
in messy writing.
The other
goblins
cheered.

With
a bad-
tempered
choking
sound, Jack
Frost stamped
his foot again,
sending a
flurry of ice chips
swirling everywhere.
When the ice chips vanished, he and the
goblins had gone.

Rachel and Kirsty cheered in triumph...and then gazed in wonder as hundreds of bright silver sparkles began shooting from Lola's magic pass and streaming down the corridor.

"Just in time," Lola breathed. "My magic will make sure everything is ready for the fashion show to run perfectly here. Which is lucky because it's due to start in just five minutes!"

Some of the magic sparkles swirled around Kirsty and Rachel and they gasped as their hair was magically styled and a touch of pink gloss was added to their lips.

62

Then, as they went out to look for Jessica, they saw that the catwalk had been fully repaired, the curtain was back up on its rail, and the audience were filing in to their seats.

"This fashion show is ready to roll," Lola said happily. "And now I should return to Fairyland and make sure that the fashion show *there* is just as perfect. Would you two like to come with me?"

Kirsty's eyes lit up immediately. She knew that time stopped in the human world while they were in Fairyland, so they wouldn't be missed for a second. "Oh yes, please," she said, just as Rachel said the same thing.

Lola smiled and waved her wand again. "Then off we go!" she cried.

# Fairy
# Fashions

In the very next moment, Rachel and Kirsty were swept up in a cloud of sparkling fairy dust and spun away from the fashion show. Soon afterwards, they felt themselves land again and the sparkles cleared to reveal that they were now inside the Great Hall of the Fairyland Palace. What was more, they were sitting in the front row of the audience, next to the King and Queen of Fairyland!

Queen Titania's eyes twinkled as she saw the girls. "Perfect timing," she said, smiling. "The show's about to start."

Rachel and Kirsty said hello to the king and queen in their politest voices, looking around excitedly to see the large catwalk and the enormous audience behind them.

Suddenly, the lights went down, and the hall was plunged into darkness. Delicate, silvery music played and a single bright spotlight shone on the centre of the stage as a figure emerged.

"It's Ruby!" whispered Kirsty with a smile as she recognised Ruby the Red Fairy, the very first fairy friend she and Rachel had ever made.

At the start of the week, when the girls had first been whisked away to Fairyland, they had sat in this very hall waiting to watch the fashion show. Back then, Jack Frost had spoiled Ruby's entrance, and Rachel now quickly crossed her fingers. Surely nothing would go wrong this time?

Ruby strode down the catwalk in a gorgeous long red dress, edged with glittering sequins. She had red roses twined through her hair, silver bangles on her wrist, and red ballet shoes, with red ribbons criss-crossing around her ankles.

"She looks so beautiful," said Rachel happily.

One after another, fairies took to the catwalk in a series of amazing outfits. This time, there were no interruptions from Jack Frost or his goblins, and definitely no Ice Blue clothes to be seen!

At the end, the audience gave a huge
round of applause, and Kirsty and
Rachel both clapped until their hands
tingled. Then Lola and the other Fashion
Fairies walked on stage holding hands
and took their bows.

"We'd just like to say," Lola began,
"that none of today's show would have
been possible without our friends, Rachel
and Kirsty – thank you, girls. Once
again, you've saved the day!"

A second round of applause broke out, and the girls blushed with joy. Oh, it was so lovely being friends with the fairies!

Queen Titania smiled at them. "We'd better send you back to your world now, as I can see you have your own special outfits to model," she said. "But before you go, let us give you a sprinkling of fairy dust, just to make you sparkle even more brightly under the catwalk lights."

She and King Oberon lightly sprinkled some of their glittering dust over the girls. "Our thanks again," King Oberon said. "And good luck with your fashion show!"

"Good luck!" chorused the Fashion Fairies, waving and smiling.

"Goodbye," Rachel said, waving back. "We hope we see you all again soon."

Queen Titania waved her wand and then, in a cloud of rainbow-coloured fairy dust, the girls went spinning away all the way back to Tippington.

Back at the fashion show, the girls saw Jessica coming towards them.

"There you are!" she cried. "We're all

set, so come and take your places in the line. I hope you're not too nervous. I know this must all be rather overwhelming for you."

Kirsty and Rachel grinned at each other. After seven adventures with the Fashion Fairies, outwitting Jack Frost and the goblins, and a whirlwind trip to Fairyland, the thought of walking down a catwalk actually seemed quite relaxing!

"I think we'll be fine," Kirsty said confidently.

"That's the spirit." Jessica smiled. "I'm

going to introduce the show now, so good luck!"

Rachel and Kirsty made their way over to the catwalk entrance. Peeping through the curtains, they could see a huge audience had gathered, including Rachel's parents in the front row.

Kirsty felt goosebumps on her arms as Jessica walked onto the stage and the audience clapped. "This is going to be great," she whispered happily.

Rachel smiled. "When we're together, things are *always* fun," she replied. "And this is the perfect way to end a *very* fashionable week with the fairies!"

Now it's time for Kirsty and
Rachel to help...

# Angelica the Angel Fairy

Read on for a sneak peek...

"The Christmas fair opens in five minutes," said Rachel Walker, her eyes dancing with excitement. "Are we ready to turn on the fairy lights?"

"Definitely!" exclaimed her best friend, Kirsty Tate.

Kirsty was staying at Rachel's house for the first half of the school holidays. The pair had enjoyed a wonderful, Christmassy week ice-skating, drinking hot chocolates and baking gingerbread. Time always seemed to rush by when Kirsty and Rachel were together!

Now it was Saturday afternoon and the friends were dressed in their Brownie uniforms. The girls in Rachel's pack had been working hard all morning – today was the day of the Tippington Brownies' Christmas Fair! Kirsty and Rachel had volunteered to run the 'winter woollies' stall, a tabletop stacked high with mittens, socks and scarves knitted in rich, festive colours.

Rachel ran to the back of the hall. When Brown Owl gave the signal, she dimmed the main lights.

Everyone closed their eyes in the darkness and counted down together. "Three, two, one…go!"

Flash!

There was a thrilling gasp, then an explosion of clapping and cheering. The Brownies had transformed Tippington's

plain old village hall into a magical
Christmas grotto! Stalls lined every wall,
each one decorated with shiny green
holly sprigs, golden baubles and scarlet
bows. Garlands of glittery lights twinkled
from the ceiling. In the kitchen, Mrs
Walker and the other Brownie mums
were busily brewing tea and plating up
Christmas treats, filling the air with the
smell of warm mince pies.

"Look at the tree." Rachel's mum
beamed. "Isn't it magical?"

Read **Angelica the Angel Fairy** to
find out what adventures are in store for Kirsty and Rachel!

# Meet the
# Fashion Fairies

If Kirsty and Rachel don't find the Fashion Fairies' magical objects, Jack Frost will ruin fashion forever!

www.rainbowmagicbooks.co.uk

Meet the fairies, play games
and get sneak peeks at
the latest books!

# www.rainbowmagicbooks.co.uk

There's fairy fun for everyone on
our wonderful website.
You'll find great activities, competitions, stories and
fairy profiles, and also a special newsletter.

Get 30% off all Rainbow Magic books at
## www.rainbowmagicbooks.co.uk

Enter the code RAINBOW at the checkout.
Offer ends 31 December 2012.

Offer valid in United Kingdom and Republic of Ireland only.

# Competition!

Here's a friend who Kirsty and Rachel met in an earlier story. Use the clues below to help you guess her name. When you have enjoyed all seven of the Fashion Fairies books, arrange the first letters of each mystery fairy's name to make a special word, then send us the answer!

## CLUES

1. This fairy is one of the Sporty Fairies.

2. In her story she helps save the Spring into Sport competition.

3. She likes wearing the colours blue and purple.

The fairy's name is _ _ _ _ _ the _ _ _ _ _ _ _ Fairy

**We will put all of the correct entries into a draw and select one winner to receive a special Fashion Fairies goody bag. Your name will also be featured in a forthcoming Rainbow Magic story!**

## Enter online now at www.rainbowmagicbooks.co.uk

No purchase required. Only one entry per child. Two prize draws will take place on 31 May 2013 and 31 August 2013. Alternatively readers can send the answers on a postcard to: Rainbow Magic Fashion Fairies Competition, Orchard Books, 338 Euston Road, London, NW1 3BH. Australian readers can write to: Rainbow Magic Fashion Fairies Competition, Hachette Children's Books, Level 17/207 Kent St, Sydney, NSW 2000. E-mail: childrens.books@hachette.com.au.
New Zealand readers should write to: Rainbow Magic Fashion Fairies Competition, 4 Whetu Place, Mairangi Bay, Auckland, NZ

# The Complete Book of Fairies

Packed with secret fairy facts
and extra-special rainbow reveals, this magical guide
includes all you need to know about your favourite
Rainbow Magic friends.

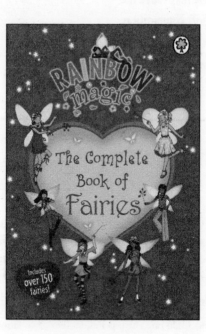

**Out Now!**